COLOUR AUSTRALIAN WILDLIFE

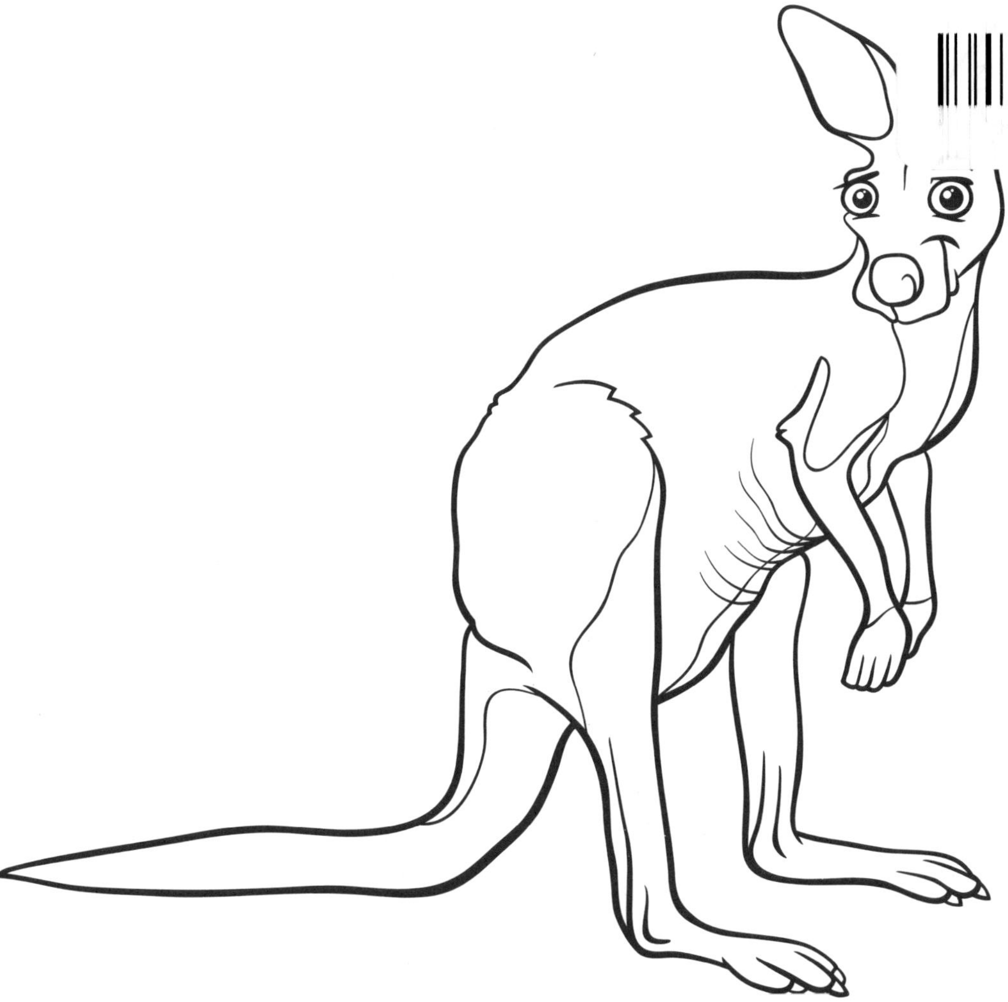

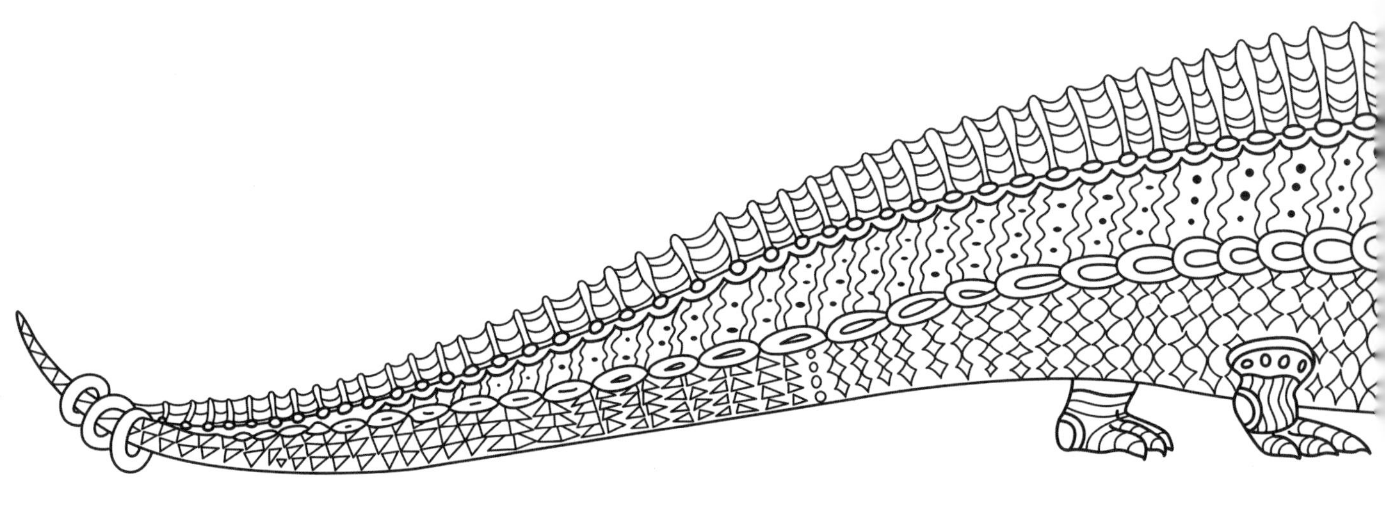

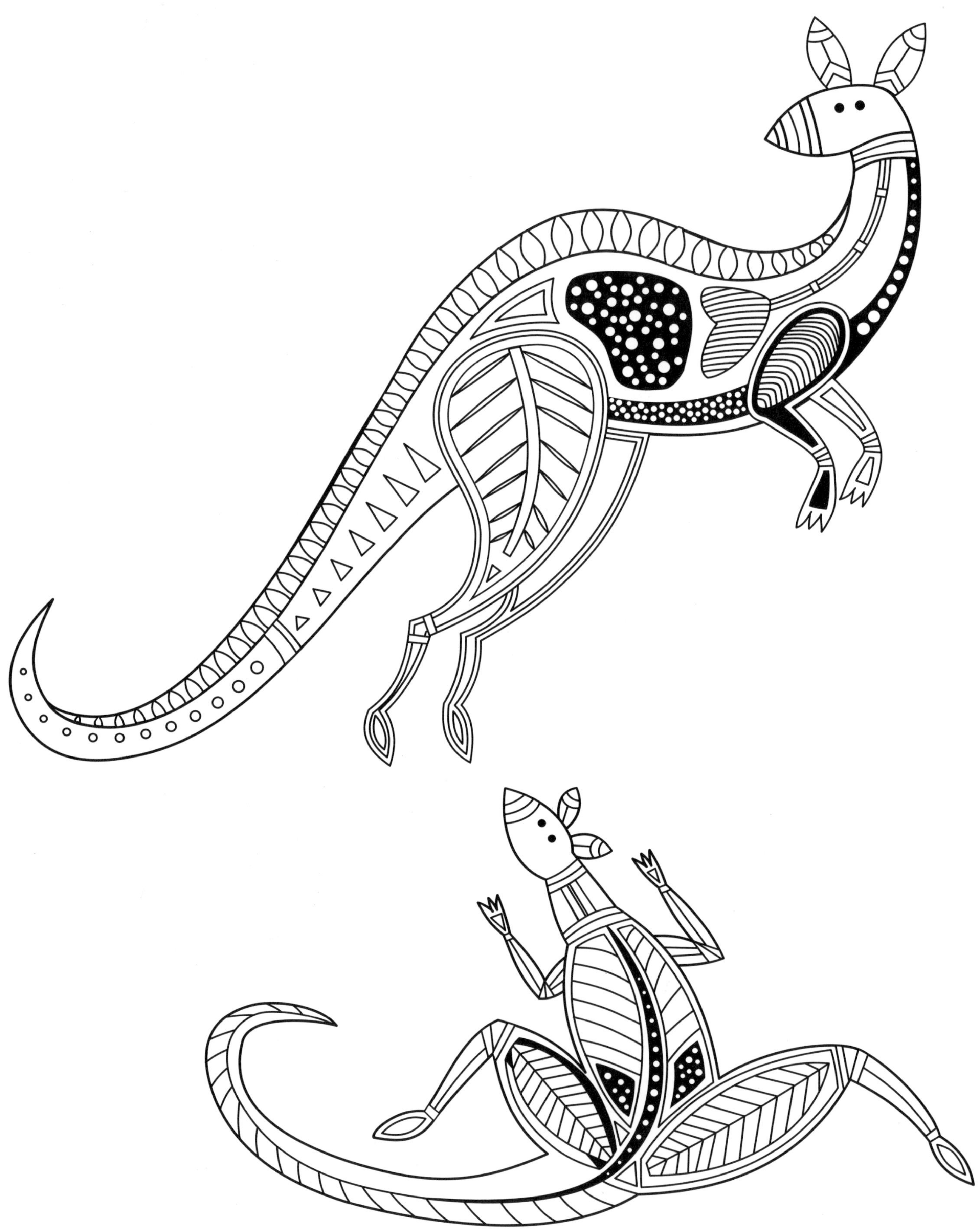

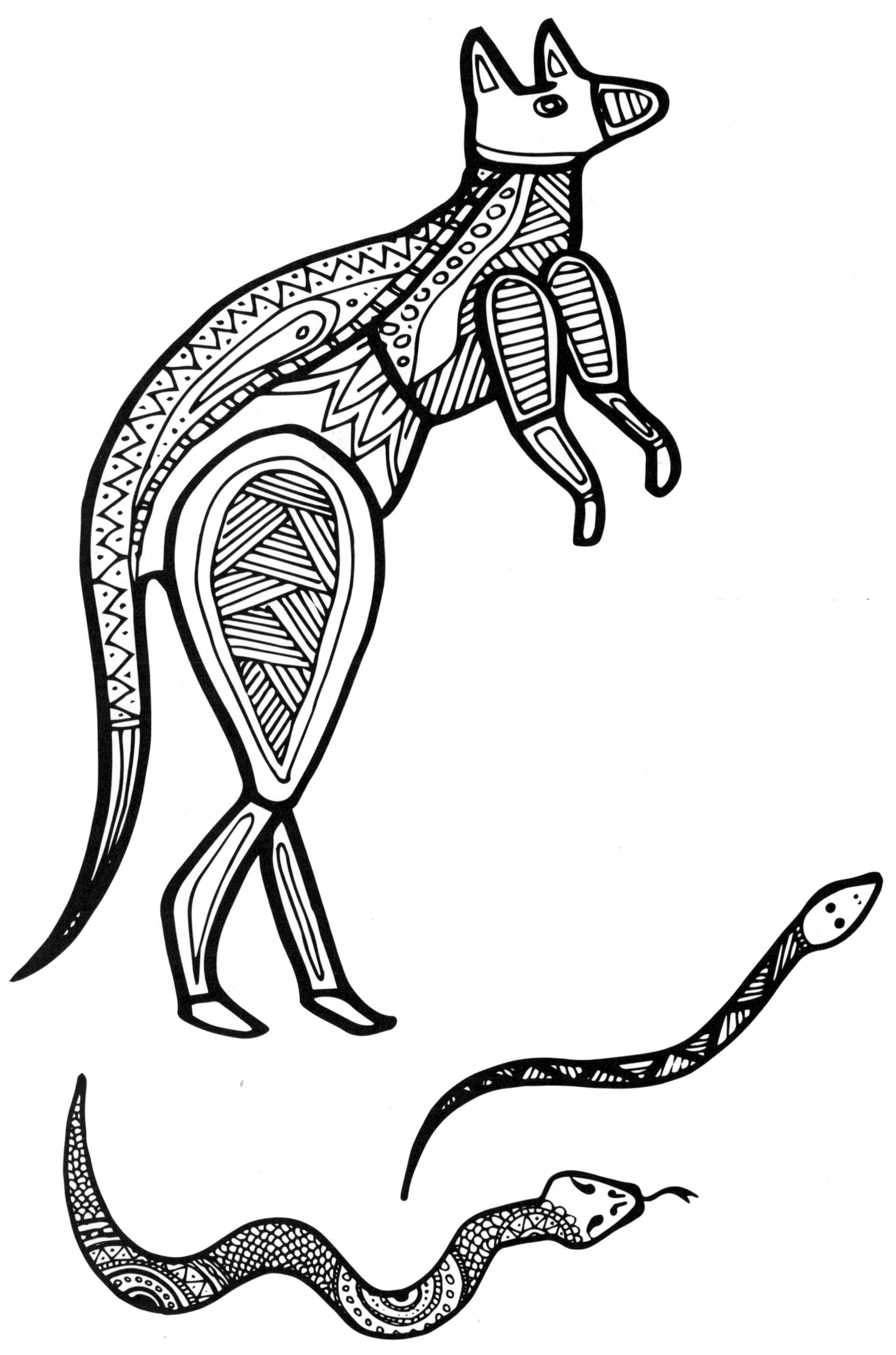

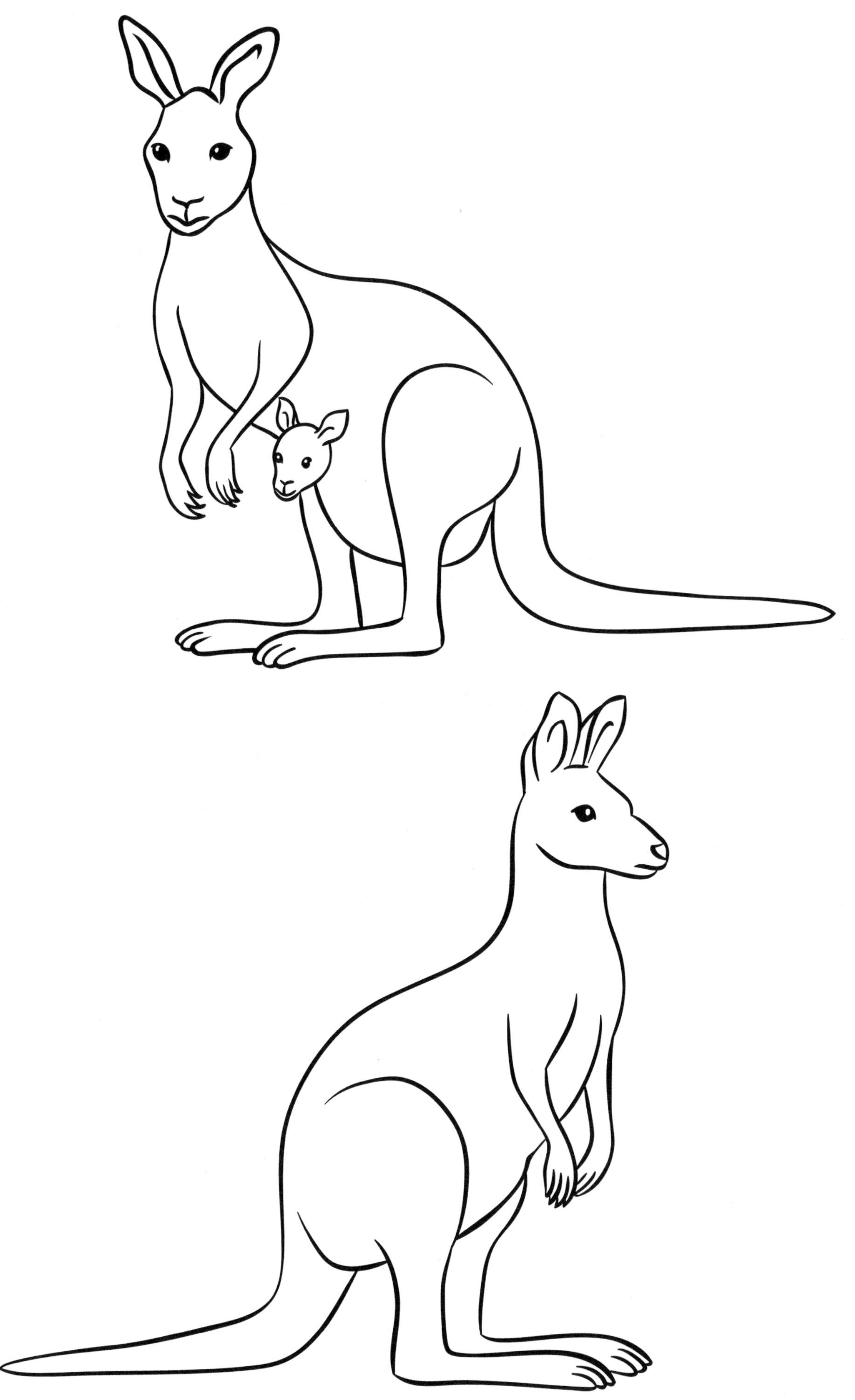

First published in 2023 by Young Reed
an imprint of Reed New Holland Publishers
Sydney

Level 1, 178 Fox Valley Road, Wahroonga, NSW 2076,
Australia

newhollandpublishers.com

A record of this book is held at the National Library of Australia.

ISBN 9781921580574

Managing Director: Fiona Schultz
Designer: Andrew Davies
Production Director: Arlene Gippert
Printed in China

10 9 8 7 6 5 4 3 2

Keep up with Reed New Holland and New Holland Publishers

ReedNewHolland
@NewHollandPublishers and @ReedNewHolland